*To Pam Horsey who loves pears
almost as much as Pamela — J.F.*

For Ellyn and Ben — B.W.

Text copyright © 2003 Jackie French.
Illustrations copyright © 2003 Bruce Whatley.

Published in the United States of America by Star Bright Books, New York.
Please visit www.starbrightbooks.com.
Published simultaneously in Australia by Koala Books.

The name Star Bright Books is a registered trademark of Star Bright
Books, Inc.
Produced by Phoenix Offset 9 8 7 6 5 4 3 2 1
Printed in Hong Kong

ISBN: 1-932065-47-4

Library of Congress Cataloging-in-Publication Data
available.

Jackie French • Bruce Whatley
Too many pears!

Star Bright Books

New York

Pamela liked pears.

Pamela liked fresh pears.

She liked pears
even more than
Amy did!

Pamela liked pears for lunch.

Pamela liked pears on picnics.

Pamela liked stewed pears
with ice cream too.

Grandpa
around t

But Pame
a womba

The next day Grandpa
opened the gate for Pamela.

"Look at all the lovely pears,
Pamela," Grandpa said.

Pamela wasn't interested.